BRAND SPANKING NEW!

Created by
Jim Jinkins

DOUG'S™

Big Shoe Disaster

Story by Jim Jinkins and Joe Aaron
Adapted by Sue Kassirer

Illustrated by Jonathan Royce
and
Irene Wu, Cheng-li Chan, Tony Curanaj, Brian Donnelly

Disney PRESS

New York

Printed in the United States of America.

FIRST EDITION

1 3 5 7 9 10 8 6 4 2

Library of Congress Catalog Card Number: 96-43612

ISBN: 0-7868-3142-1

Original characters for "The Funnies" developed by Jim Jinkins and Joe Aaron

Doug Funnie

Skeeter Valentine

Beebe Bluff

Doug's World

Roger Klotz

Porkchop

Patti Mayonnaise

One morning Doug decided to go for a walk. But before he had gone very far, he stepped in a puddle. And his left foot got wet.

"Whaddaya know, Porkchop," he said to his dog. "My shoe sprang a leak! Looks like I need a new pair of shoes."

Porkchop looked down at Doug's shoes. They *were* getting old. The laces were in knots and Doug's toes *were* sticking out.

So the two of them headed for the Four Leaf Clover Mall.

Doug and Porkchop walked into Shoes 'n Shoes.
They looked at lots of shoes.

Doug tried on boat shoes.
But they made him seasick.

He tried on banana slippers.
But they were way too slippery.

He tried on Swiss cheese shoes.
But they had more holes than his
old shoes.

He tried on house shoes.
But they were much too roomy.

He tried on tuna shoes.
But they just made him think of Patti Mayonnaise.

Doug was about to give up.
Then he spotted another pair of shoes.
They looked a lot like his old shoes, but bigger.
"Hey, Porkchop, look at those!" said Doug.

He tried them on.
They fit just right.
And they looked just right.

"But wait," said Doug. His heart sank.

"Everyone's wearing fancy shoes, Porkchop. Nobody gets plain old shoes anymore. If I get the gray-and-white shoes, I'm scared the kids will laugh at me."

Porkchop shrugged and looked down at the floor.

Doug didn't want to be laughed at, so he decided to get the tuna shoes.

"Why don't you wear your new shoes home," said the saleswoman, putting Doug's old shoes in the shoe box.

As Doug and Porkchop walked home, they ran
into some friends.

"Hey, Doug!" said Skeeter, pointing to Doug's
Shoes 'n Shoes bag. "New shoes! Let's see them!"

"Uh, sure," said Doug.

But before Doug could say that the new shoes were on his feet, Roger grabbed the bag and dumped out the old shoes. The kids stared at them.

"Cool! The worn look! Like washed-denim jeans! Really cool!" they said at once. "Do they have any more?"

And the kids ran off to Shoes 'n Shoes.

Doug looked down at his tuna shoes.
His friends hadn't even noticed them.
They liked his *old* shoes.
They thought *those* were his new shoes!

When Doug and Porkchop got home, Doug thought about his old shoes.

He thought about his new shoes.

He thought about what the kids had said.

He thought about them looking for shoes like his old shoes.

He looked at Porkchop. The lucky guy didn't even *wear* shoes.

Finally Doug decided to return the new shoes.

"Why should I keep them?" he said to Porkchop. "They weren't even the ones I wanted. Maybe I can wear my old ones a little longer."

So Doug took off the new shoes.
He put his old shoes back on and put the new shoes in the bag.

On the way to the store Doug bumped into some more kids.

"Hey, Doug. New shoes! From my favorite store!" said Beebe Bluff. "Can we see them?"

"Well, uh," said Doug, and he stubbed the toe that was sticking out of his old shoes.

The shoe box fell on the ground, and out fell the tuna shoes.

Beebe, Connie, and Chalky all stared at the shoes in wonder.

"They're faboo!" said Beebe. "I've got to have a pair!"

Before Doug could speak, the kids ran off.

Doug knew where they were going—to Shoes 'n Shoes.

Doug and Porkchop turned around and headed home.
Back in his room, Doug got out his journal and began writing.

Dear Journal:
    *The kids liked my old
shoes when they thought
they were new. They didn't
even look at my new shoes
when they thought they
were old. Then they did like
my new shoes when they
saw they were new. But
the shoes I really want are
the gray-and-white shoes
that are back in the store.*

The next day Doug knew just what to do.

He went back to the shoe store and returned the tuna shoes, and he bought the gray-and-white shoes.

Doug was nearly home when a voice called out.

"Doug, watch out! A puddle!"

But it was too late. He had already stepped in the puddle.

"I tried to warn you in time so that you wouldn't get your brand-new shoes all wet," said Patti Mayonnaise.

"That's OK, Patti," said Doug with a big smile. "Actually, this is great!"

"What's great?" Patti asked.

"Not only do my new shoes fit right and look right, they don't leak. And do you know what that makes these shoes?" asked Doug.

"What?" asked Patti.

"Perfect!" And Doug smiled.